ABASTAV

SUR REAL

SOMA AMRIT BHABANI

PARTRIDGE
A Penguin Random House Company

To order additional copies of this book, contact
Partridge India
000 800 10062 62
www.partridgepublishing.com/india
orders.india@partridgepublishing.com

Acknowledgement

FIRST OF ALL, I MUST ACKNOWLEDGE THE GOD, UNLESS HIS BLESSING, THIS JOB WAS NOT POSSIBLE FOR ME.

SECONDLY, I AM THE MOST GRATEFUL TO THE PATRIDGE PUBLISHING LIMTED, SPECIALLY TO MR. JAMES CLIFFORD—SENIOR EDITOR OF THE HOUSE. WITHOUT THEIR CONSTANT INSPIRATION, COOPERATION AND GUIDANCE, I CAN NOT BE THE ACHIEVER.

AND ABOVE ALL, I MUST CONVEY MY THANKS TO THE MANY FRIENDS OF MY CITY AND OUTSIDE, WHO HAS ENCOURAGED AND HELP ME TO PUBLISH MY WORK.

AND ALSO, MY ADVANCE 'DHANYABAD' TO THE READERS AND CRITICS FOR SPENDING SOME TIME FOR THE SAKE OF THIS 'ABASTAV' (SUR REAL) STORY.

—SOMA AMRIT BHABANI

DEDICATION

The fiction novel Abastav (Sur Real) is dedicated to my cyber friends for whom my life has turned up and speed up.

The introduction of a new team of boys from earth (sampan group) and their mannerism is the effect of that 4 year long relation.

—Soma Amrit Bhabani

DISCLAIMER

The characters and incidences of this book Abastav (sur real) is totally imaginary.

Any resemblance found anywhere within the text is merely a coincidence.

Soma Amrit Bhabani

PREFACE

Abastav (Sur Real) is a value added fiction novel.

It is unique for world literature—a high tech space colony story.

The incidents, scenario, dress, and gadgets are all based on scientific theory. Many are well established, some under the research work of the author. Not to make any discontinuity, the trade marks are not included in the text. The list of such topics under research work is attached.

Abastav is a wrap type fiction novel. The space adventure to a satellite named Neo covers a fantasy, which is a classical relativity love story. Here, the time of the two part of the story are different. The space expedition is a space tour of some grown up boys at 2500 A.D. and the fantasy is of 2100 A.D.

Abastav is the fourth fiction of the author's space colony sequel, starting from 'Antariksha'. For that, some terms are in continuation from the previous. But those will not hamper the flow of the story.

As, Abastav is written for those of any age, having a passion for science and technology, the heavy dictionary words are not included and written in very simple English language, easy understandable for those also whose mother tongue or schooling is not in English.

The author expects comments and criticism from the readers.

Soma Amrit Bhabani

CHAPTER ONE

white desert

ERA—2500 A.D. PLACE—NEO

Call of the lips
  irresistably took me to the pole,
    swinging,
      vibrating,

FAU IS SINGING AND DANCING

FAU—A big fatty penguin.

Miles after miles view is white. Within that white desert, the penguin is dancing over white floor before a small hill—like a blackish statue of a girl with white gown.

Now, it is 9-30 a.m.
He continues his dancing. Alone. No one is seen over the white.

Signal interpreted by heart
Response due for meeting.
Call of the lips s s

A group of penguins in same form but with smaller size enter within the song. Hear for some time.

One of them broke the queue, come between the group and Fau.

He is Nou. He looks at Fau and then the statue.

*   *   *

The scene is changed. The time is 12 noon.
Another penguin, almost alike but scrutiny will find some difference.
Come running, hide himself beyond the statue, sit on ground and started to cry.
He is RONA. Have a habit to cry here and there . . . now and then.

*   *   *

Now this is the evening time—as per the local standard time, but intensity of light over the whole space is same as before.

Exactly same as the morning.

Another penguin, similar to those before, with some difference in length and breadth come in slow walking mood to the statue.

His looking is totally scientific, examined the statue by his eyes.

He is BAYNA (nagging for his demand).

He is passionate with his research. For which he is here.

CHAPTER TWO

NEO—the venue

ONCE WILL BE THE TIME.

F ew years ago, about 2400 a.d., a group of human being leave the earth.
They were not happy with the crowd, the pollution and with the world.

The space program which is very well known to all you, make a quick review.

In 19th century it was started to conquer the space.

In 20th century, it goes to the boom. The human being overcome the gravity of the earth. In the middle of the century, the space stations were formed. Along with, they began to walk over the other planets of the solar system. The land of moon was covered by them earlier.

The search of some other intellectual species were started simultaneously. That time it was through signals.

They became happy even if they can find an animal or insect there.

But no hope. Till date there is no sign of life is found from north to south or from east to west of the solar system.

In between these years, in 22nd century, their tour program was at Jupiter.

In 23rd and 24th century, they made the search, not only for life but to make the colony at the satellites of Jupiter and Saturn.

In 25th century, they found IIO, one satellite of Jupiter, suitable for living artificially.

They made the colony at IIO, facility achieved day by day—those are different stories. You will find that in 'Antariksha'.

Now, in 26th century, a group of youth—the second generation of IIO citizens discovered NEO—quite human friendly satellite of Jupiter, which is now under their research.

First time, this group of boys faced a lot of trouble, a long fight also happened there for the land. And ultimately, they won, permitted to carry on their project. This was the story of 'Amrit'.

This is the second time, they landed over neo.

The story is happening now and here.

SAB/SR-1

CHAPTER THREE

Romance

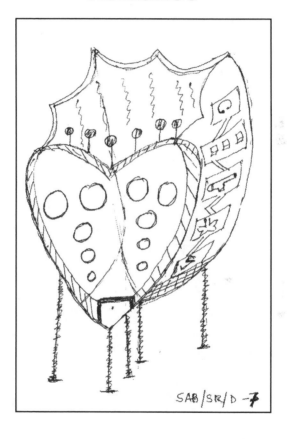

SAB/SR/D -7

R omance—the super galaxy vehicle.

Romance was designed in 23rd century.

It is powered by nuclear battery.

From any side, romance is like a heart shaped box. A very very large box.

With a no. of legs beyond.

In 21st century, the space vehicles were powered by solar energy. But during long distance expeditions, the shadow regions started to move.

The satellites are covered by their masters, or sun light has loses its intensity due to distance by inverse law of candela.

And the sun was defeated there in power game. Necessity needs the improvement. The nuclear battery took the place. The major advantage is the volume decrease, as the wings are optional.

For a fly in atmosphere, the volume expansion is an advantage; but in space you must squinze yourself. Streamline figure—required to cut the air is not a must.

The skin protection system has improved for the space vehicles everyday. Romance has special cover to ignore named and unnamed different rays flowing over the space. As like the UV—ultraviolet, Many of them have damaging attitude.

The inside of Romance, as usual, have the cubicles. The telescope room, the microscope room, the signal room— with all other technical rooms there is the kitchen, the dining and the rest rooms. Except those, romance has own security system with the highest 26th century gadgets.

Romance is the special expedition vehicle was made by persons of IIO. It was once damaged during the last adventure. Goes beyond hope to be cured. But it was done. And now it swim over a large no. of light years to revisit NEO.

The hat antennas at the roof—are always hearing. Even a whisper reach their ear(specially if it is something spicy!). The red balls at their end has the eagles' sight.

CHAPTER FOUR

the Romance group

DANCE TIME

Love   like   pity   hate

    Adore   kiss   marriage   friend

        Love   like

Fau—the healthy penguin is dancing, the thinners are singing with making a round around it.

They are—

Nau—have a habit to tell 'now' in between all sentence.

Pau—a bit more intelligent of them.

Hou—a bit less intelligent, take some time to understand, and within the inertia of brain, he must make the question 'how?'

Tou—a bit calm, does work with concentration,

Kou—the wise man of the group

Mou—have a sharp eyesight

Sou—the monitor of the group. Older of them . . . like to cook stories in leisure.

This group is the young space scientist group of IIO. Romance carry them over the space.

All of them have different assigned duties.
Nou, Hou assist Sou to chemical experiments.
Pou remains busy with the atmosphere.
Tou throws and catches signal.
Mou is for watching the zone.

But the most important is Fau. It is a biobot. In previous expedition to Neo—another robot was with them—Chou; who died at that time. The next generation become the new member.

They are now at a small gap within their job with Fau as the entertainer.

CHAPTER FIVE

NEO

ORBITS

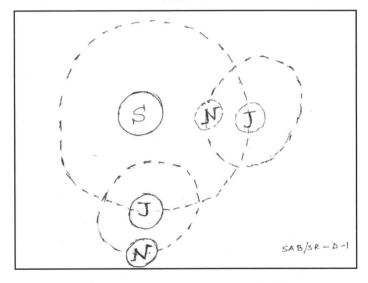

SAB/SR — D-1

Neo—the satellite of Jupiter discovered few century ago i.e. in 23ʳᵈ or 24ᵗʰ.

The citizens of IIO—another satellite of the Jupiter discovered it.

The topor sheet of Neo was developed slowly day by day by them.

Firstly they felt hopeless and helpless as it has no atmosphere like all other members of the solar system except the Earth.

No water, no air—another sigh of human race.

But as those people already had set up the colony against all odds and those small lacks of the heavenly body IIO, they did not care.

Their expeditions continued.

They found the most uncommon.

Neo has no axial rotation. And its size is much larger than IIO or many other satellites—a hundred times than the moon.

And the result? It has day and night for six months about according to the watch and calendar system of the Earth.

Six month day and six month night.

During the last visit to Neo, the Romance group was resided at the lighter part—full of strong Sun. And after long search, they found the 'RASA TREE'—tree like structure who supply high density water, sweet in taste, uses Siphon formula to rasa supply. After a long war with another group of human species from Earth, the Romance group won the match.

This time, before starting from IIO, they decided to land and home at the darker side. Now they are there. With the white statue within the white desert.

Oh, yes! They have eliminate the dark with their nuclear generator arrangement. It is a portable small nuclear reactor—quite larger than the nuclear battery which, they use for their vehicles.

But, the main problem is the temperature. It goes much beyond their thermometer.

So cold so cold so cold.

Minimum five times colder than Syberia.

Within romance, they are at room temperature, I mean at tolerable temperature.But, they have to work outside. Don't get afraid. Theylanded with preparation. To bit the heat.

CHAPTER SIX

FAU

SAB/SR/D —2

Kiss—the hit or miss

Fau is dancing before the girl statue.

Fau—the most important member of Romance. The best friend of Sau, Pau, Nou. But he is not like them. He is a biobot. A robot with some biological proceses.

Fau has the metabolic system like human being. It takes veg food. Internally it has the system to digest it. Like human being this food gives energy to Fau. And it can make an output of solid. This is a mechanical process.

The control unit of Fau is a Cadberry operating system. It can recognize its known person. Its memory preserve the identity and some words for that person. By this process he always conduct with the Romance members.

They have the password—the song.

The few century ago, the cadberry operating system is introduced for the modern generation robots. Fau can talk in the human voice. The internal stored dubbing chip is used for that.

In one word, you should not call Fau as 'it', rather' he 'is better for him.

And have self protecting system. His collar. The penguin dress which he wear every time has a special collar. Fau shake it in a special pose and the unwanted person will find a kick.

Whenever, Fau saw something which he never saw before, he makes an alert call to his friends. Fau is the next generation of chau. Chau could not sing nor can talk. But he had strength. Chau died at the last time arrival of romance at neo. After his sad demise, Fau from IIO's lab joined to them. His birth was there, and grown up also there. His training was completed when he joined to the group.

The best of his properties is one, which charmed everyone is he can sing and can dance.

Now he is busy to shrug his collar to make a hole within the white sand.

The duty allotted to him.

CHAPTER SEVEN

romance on duty

Not only fau, all of romance group are at their work.

Pau is busy with the search antennas. Within the last five hundred years, the space communication has improved many times. Upto the twenty first century, the communication was limited to the nearer zone of the earth. Through satellite system. But as the intelligent race started to cross the boundary to settle themselves to other planets, the need changes. Now earth can contact up to the Saturn. Through the space station relay centers.

Pau is talking with the guardians at IIO. It's his daily routine. To sent the progress report there. And to take their advice.

Sau, the chief researcher examining the data taken by the assistants yesterday.

Kau is with the cameras . . . the security system—for near and far.

Mou is the guard now.

Nou, Hau Tau with Fau are at out of romance. They are investigating the ground of the land. It is all white like the ice. But, they have tried to melt it. Very high melting point. Cold as ice but the sand like element.

The group is using the high frequency coherence wave to drill to find the lower layer.

If here was the ground like earth—Tau is full of sorrow.

And if here was the water—Nou. As now, they had to bring water from the other part Neo. Some stock also they have from Neo.

Fau is very serious about his work. Trying to make hole to the base of girl statue. The statue with the background support is quite large. It is like a covered cave. Fau wants to enter within it. His size is larger than other all. He started to drill.

Adore   adore   more   more

Fau takes some energy from the rest gap. The other three also joined. Romance is at their view. Standing at a distance.

If by chance, this space have a storage of water. They are searching the underground here and there. We have to reach at a larger depth. But how? Hou is thinking.

The day is at its end. It's time to return to their romance.

Fau is a better dancer. They clapped to his dance. The clap make no sound. The space is a no sound zone. Obviously. They are on their return way.
You can visualize another three dots moving towards the girl statue.
They are Rona, Khayna and Bayna.

They are from the earth. By their vehicle 'Sampan'.

CHAPTER EIGHT

Sampan

7   8   ALL RIGHT

Rona, Bayna, Khayna, Jayna and Aayna—five members of another space vehicle Sampan over the desert land.

After the last war for the rasa tree, the Iio made a pact with the citizens of the earth. For peace program. They decided team from both the sectors will continue their research program with some distinct rules. Without making any harm to other.

Sampan is almost a space vehicle like the romance, acting as for transport and camping both.

Jayna is their team leader.

Rona, Bayna, khayna are marching towards the statue.

As usual, Rona is depressed with his known environment.

Khayna who has a habit of thinking about food always is walking against his will. He very much dislike this research works.

Only Bayna is chocking their activity.

He himself put to observe the statue and send the other two to the desert to collect the samples. Aayna is home guard today.

Will you marry sona? Khayna asked.

Rona, yet not decided. He only wants to leave this place.

See, here is no sky—he told Khyna. No blue sky.

No black sky also, Khyna make him remind the clouds.

And no rain—rona

Hence no rainy days-Khyna

No green—Rona

Not a little bit—Khyna

Some times they collect the ice dust. They are also in the penguin dress.

A collection from the Romance . . . in many ways they are dependent on Romance.

Bayna is making notes over the statue. The dimension first.

Aayna—the other member joined them at the middle. Walk the whole ground in supervising mood. Jayna depends on Aayna. He is not light as Rona and Khayna. Stand to hear those two.

And all the delicious—Khyna with a sigh.

CHAPTER NINE

the clock

The clock is at the neck of the girl. Like a pendant.

Bayna look at the watch. 10 hours of sampan A.M.—the clock is saying.

Romance and sampan both the group maintain their time with this watch.

The size is quite large. Within the sight from a large distance.

The time is by default fixed in synchro with the earth.

This part of Neo is always at night and always at day for the power.

The calibration is made as per need. It shows the 12 hours for Romance, when the Romance members are allowed to roam over the desert. The next twelve hours is for sampan.

The clock is a simple atomic clock. Bayna thought, if this statue was not here, how the clock was placed. They have all their own, even Fau also has his, but you can not run two watches at same pace.

Bayna look for other two. Generally, he likes to work alone. Bayna Jayna add them many times. Must be gossiping, yes, off course. Bayna found them. Call them to drill the knee of the statue.

Another two hours they have. Bayna wants to win. They are in competition with the romance group.

   8 7 8   all right—Rona Aayna Khayna are closer.

7 8 7 8   keep quiet—Aayna stopped them.

They started to finish the routine.
Jayna from sampan was watching them.

Now, this is the night time for romance. Members are at rest. One or two are alert and awake to guard their camp. Rest are sleeping. After some time it will be morning.

Sampan is about half a mile from the statue. Generally, two groups avoid each other.

The four is packing their bag and instruments.

CHAPTER TEN

special jacket

The members have returned. It is their evening time.

Two of them are engaged in dining.

At Iio, when the human group made the colony, the food were supplied from the earth. At regular interval, they shuttle to their home land to take the ration.

But, day by day, the system improved there.

And, the biggest invention they made about three hundred years ago. They completed the food manufacturing machine. To prepare carbohydrates by themselves, from the gaseous in gradients. The Iio people become the primary food producer. That's another story.

The romance group take their food from the Iio stock. They carry it in the amount for the camp days.

Pau look at Tau and Nau. No, the dinner will be late. He remain to continue his work. Examining their life jacket. Mau is as usual silent worker, with sharp watch.

The Penguins. In the twenty first century, research was made over them. How they can bear so cold. How they can swim in ice water etc etc.

Special interest was to their wings. It was found that the speciality is in the layers of their feather.

When it was decided, the romance group will land in the darker zone, the super cool zone, the question arose about their uniform. What it will be?

Search brings back the century ago result. The penguin jackets was tailored. The special poly fibre is used here. The internal layers are like the feathers of the penguins. Just for fun, the tailor shape the jackets also like the penguins. Various accessories attached as per their need for the work and for the security.

Pau is concentrated to the collars of Fau. It is very important for them. The left can break your hand. The right is to alert them. By a gentle finger strike Fau makes ring the alarm bell within the romance. Telling that some unknown is nearby. And the left? When his finger strike it, his legs are straight. One will think it is dancing pose, before he fall to the ground.

CHAPTER ELEVEN

Bayna

Bayna is the brain of the sampan group.

He is very imaginative in nature.

He likes to do school level mathematics.

He likes discovery.

He likes competition.

When he heard that Sou Pou is making expedition to Neo, his ego awake. He demands one such group from earth must visit there.

But, they are handicapped. Handicapped in many ways.

They communicate with Iio. Iio agreed to lend them sampan. Basically, sampan is used at Iio for the seniors during their holiday galaxy tour.

Sampan landed at Neo few days after the Romance.

But, the temperature was their out of imagination. The available winter dress of the Eskimos also failed.

They returned.

Till now, Iio people depend on Earth for their life. So, Bayna and group get the penguin dress.

Now, Bayna is looking outside from the window of sampan. And calculates over his slate.

The force of attraction. His mind is diverted. For the English words.

Force of attraction, hum. Neo may, not may, must have a lot. But, picture of a girl comes to his mind, a girl of the world. Nothing, no force of attraction.

The string of his thinking is like this—the big bang the sun and its planetary system the red planet the earth the Jupiter

Then why the Jupiter has not the atmosphere

That girl her nose that is the problem point but other characteristics

Gravitation why I am thinking about gravity only.

The ice dust actually what is it.

Face cutting no the main point is intellect blant type

Rather, the girl statue, has—thought goes within. Bayna is filling some attraction.

CHAPTER TWELVE

Ferry

FERRY TOUR

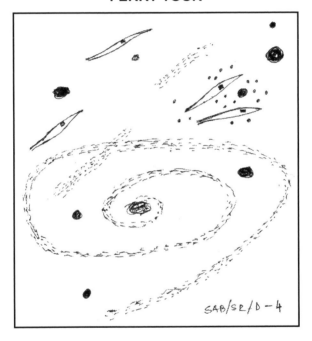

Nau and Pau passes a black hole through its two sides. With a enormous velocity.

The other make a combined laugh. Laugh of win.

The romance group is on a holiday mood. They are making round at the sky over Neo.

Ferry—the car for this purpose.

Ferry is a single seater galaxy cab. Powered by small nuclear battery.

The shape is like a flying bird. Made of light metal fibre.

This is their driving practice time. They enjoy it very much.

Simultaneously, they are doing something.

These black holes become their headache. Their means the Iio people.

It is discovered that the internal matters of the black holes are very costly.

And the earth people are crazy about those.

The romance group found the space shuttle to move around these holes.

These heavenly bodies were discovered in the nineteenth century. That time it was taken not of interest. The scholars were eager to know the facts of other astro bodies like the dwarfs, pulsars etc.

Recently, the scenario changes. Someone predicts that the matters within the black holes will be precious metals. It may be. As the low valued matters have generally low melting points. If any metal or non-metal can preserve its self within the hole, probability is to be costly.

Many space shuttle have damaged, even finished for those crazy adventure, till the need has no limit.

After some turns over the head of neo in these days, the other lands become familiar. The Romance group named them also.

No, today, no other vehicle is at their view.

They have a duty to give those earth people a caution.

They were flying like a folk of birds.

Fau can not drive. He is at Romance with Sau. For security also.

They never keep Romance alone.

CHAPTER THIRTEEN

sampan evening

Plutonic love!

Ayna tell Rona. It is your plutonic love. All are at their dining table.

What's that? Rona is curious.

Aayna explained. Love is two type—one way and two way. Yours is of first type.

A psychological problem—khayna whispered.

No response from Sona forced Rona to leave the earth.

But he is trying from the vacuum.

Sampan has a different menu from the Romance. They have brought rice wheat etc. and cooked them. Not like the semi artificial food of the Romance group. They have the' ready to eat' prepared by human photosynthesis mechanism.

Rona is drafting a letter to Sona with the help of other two.

Bayna is far away from them, though sitting beside. He always sit at the window seat. His imagination already spread its wings. He is viewing future Neo.

Actually, the original word was platonic. Plato was a thinker once upon a time. The love without any physical presence was called platonic love.

And plutonic?

When it is in space, it will be plutonic.

Khayna add to Aayna—and when it is nearer to Pluto.

We must find something, something new, Bayna determined. He will not allow the romance group to win. And the girl statue—there must be something, why something, many thing precious.

He had heard about this statue for last few years. Almost from his childhood.

It is not his liking—they are back in technology. The Iio people are far advanced. In many ways they have to depend on Iio. It is not his liking. But now, no other way. Better we want to bit them here.

He take some rice, others are almost at the end. A name, we must give her a name . . . he tried to find a name suitable.

Uki, hum, it will fit her. Uki—ice in Japanese.

Chapter fourteen

Uki

U ki Uki Uki—the romance group is around the white statue.

Now all they call her as Uki.

Fau likes her. Show his dance her.

Kau changed his steps day before. Now he is in waltz steps.

Nau Pau Hou are with their drill machine.

Last night they were discussing about this statue.

Is it a pyramid? Pau asked Sau.

Sau's answer was negative. No, pyramid is a man made structure. It shows the advanced knowledge of the ancient Egypt. A land of the Africa continent.

You know the Aryans were the most developed race. They resided at different places in Asia. Their knowledge of astrology astronomy and mathematics astonished us even today.

But when communication started through land and water way, the total view came in front. The shape and size of the Earth, the continents gradually became known to all.

Very very old civilizations discovered. The pyramids rank themselves within the seven wonder of the world. For its geometry, for its volume, for its purpose, for its residents.

I know, the cone. It is to disguise from the storm, the sand storm—Nou.

And the height, it is of the height of twenty man—Sau added. The question was how the stones went such a height.

How?—Hou asked. Simply by a crane.

That time thousand and thousand years ago, that time no machine was over the earth. Man was the only machine. Kau points out.

The slants help them . . . you know the difference of net work done between carrying a mass m to a height h direct and slant path—Sau remind them.

What a enormous energy loss, even in slant path, Pau exclaimed.

Nothing dear, nothing, to keep one's name for over five thousand year.

And will be, will be so long earth will not die.

CHAPTER FIFTEEN

Pyramid

Bayna is in continuation of his brain wave.

Others finished there diner and went to sleep.

Bayna takes the duty of the guard. He has many thing to think.

Pyramid!

Uki may be the pyramid. May be it is also made by man. Even by super man. May be here was living more intellectual than man.

Bayna makes the self defence. The civilization destroyed many times over earth. People of one era did not know their existence. Modern history brings those in front of us.

Here also may be like that.

Bayna's mind enters within the pyramid. Scenes found from his learning materials.

May be, it was built by some king. The treasures he found this and that corner within Uki.

Bayna is good of drawing. He started to copy the statue or the cave or the man made structure.

The height is about 20 ft. when they stand nearer, they are only at the base. That means the base is of the height of 6 ft. Bayna 's height.

Byna looks through the window.

Fau is now at his position.

He dislikes it. He dislikes it very much.

He shift his eyes. And continues to sketch. If something found from the dimensions. Something hidden.

Khayna wakes up. With sleeping eye, come closer to Bayna.

Bayna knows his destination is the fridge. At least some rasa.

Do you want to walk through the stones? Khayna asked.

Aayna in between time joined. No he is thinking of pyramid-speak with a view to the straight lines over the sketch of Uki.

There may be the dead bodies—khayna in fear.

Not the simple type dead bodies, they are mummy—Aayna make him clear.

Dead body is dead body, of us or of mummy's—Khayna sticks to his argument. He dislike to hear about dead body at night.

At night!

CHAPTER SIXTEEN

Smell

Love like pity hate

And no date here no date

The romance group is on action.
The others are using the machinery.
Only Fau is exception.
He is dancing around Uki.
And at a regular interval strike his left collar.
Some ice dust falls on the ground.

Water fuel or anything new—not available at earth, they are searching.

But the stones are very hard, very large. It seems to them as the whole ground is all total a single piece.

Pau is within the romance. With sharp eyes over the monitors. Different data is over the screens. Mau is at round, surrounding the camp.

The detectors are always at work.

The signal detector is engaged for known, unknown unseen waves. They can reach at romance from the earth, from the space, from other planets and their satellites and obviously from Iio.

The temperature detector, the moisture detector, the pressure detector—all are keeping the internal atmosphere of Romance stable. Change of any physical quantity damage the health of vehicle and the members.

The smell detector—kept as a security device. Have specimen smells of the members. Will alert if any unknown smell comes to its nose.

Sau is busy with the analysis of the ice dust. He tries to bring the temperature of the white sand at Romance temperature.

He comes to the door, with the long sight lens to see the positions of the other members. Fau is not at his view. Probably at the other side. Nou, Hou, Tou are looking for soft region over the statue.

Pou is shakened. The smell detector rings him.

The detector probe is with Fau.

Some unknown smell is plotting a curve over the monitor of the smell detector.

CHAPTER SEVENTEEN

HT

The high tension. Pau looks for the remote. Remote for the high tension of Fau.

Sweet smell! Pau just have find it.

The smell detector probe is at the button of Fau. Like a rose on the coat.

Sound or smell nothing move in this land. Due to absence of the air medium. To get the smell, the romance group arranged the instrument from Iio before their take off.

Only the high frequency waves can flow. The probe is a sensor to convert the smell to a high frequency wave.

Good smell has high frequency. Bad smell has lower than those.

Actually, smell is also a signal for our body, a neuro signal. Enters through our nose and detected by our brain.

The detector part of the smell meter is before Pau. The frequency tells him—it is a sweet smell.

Fau, for his daily life, generally needs low power. To walk, to talk, to dance, to look etc. this power is generated by the burning of his food.

But, his heart is high tension. A nuclear battery is placed there like the pacemaker producing high value of power. Variable in magnitude, variable in frequency.

It is he use for his high tension expression, to throw his leg during the wings spread.

Pau make it on.

Fau spread its wings . . . like a hand fan. Some dust fall on the ground from the statue.

With his wings, he continues his waltz. The other eyes are towards him.

With a praise at their eyes. Fau is as dancing with his fiansee.

Pau in keen observation. The intensity has increased.

It must be some gas coming out from the statue. Pau verifies whether poisonous or not. No, all are ok. No bad effects till now.

After two three round, confirmed Pau call Sau.

The intensity is not increasing now. Sau check by switching the HT.

Yes, it is from there. From the statue.

The body odour of Uki!

Chapter eighteen

smell of jealousy

CAD berry, he is just a cad berry, Bayna makes himself understand.

He is angry. Very much angry. Anger of jealousy.

The smell is detected at sampan also.

Fau becomes the inventor.

Bayna call him as cad berry, for the operating system of the biobot.

That day, when all are at sleep, the smell came to the meter of sampan.

Bayna was guard. He silently keep watch over the matter.

He found the increase in intensity, with the dance. Dance of the robot. Phooh!

But how? Bayna and other are always nearer to Uki. No smell found.

Romance is generous. Otherwise they did not found these informations.

Their smell detector is a loan element. Sampan is the borrower.

But, he had seek the source hiding.

And, that is the problem.

Next morning, he showed the data. Jayna told him to leave the matter.

The others are also with same opinion.

They do n't like any problem. They will pass some days here, will take some data and will return to earth. It will be a excursion to tell.

Bayna has to do many thing.

He forced the other.

He will find the mystery before romance.

Deceision was made. Aayna Khayna Rona will make a deep dig with high power drill.

Byna will be at the smell detector. Jayna, firstly opposes.

Probably, they became naughty. They are teesing us. Jayna points. The smell, Nau Hau may carry something with them. How are you sure that it is from Uki?

Bayna wins as usual. With his logic.

Smell is out. After hours labour.

Smell of rotten egg.

Chapter nineteen

Love

S weet smell for the Romance, and bad smell for us! Khayna's out of understanding.

No, it is not understandable to any one of them.

Even for the brilliant Bayna is also.

It is the credit of the CAD berry—Aayna.

CADberry? Bayna is thinking. He got no scope to examine the biobot by him. But is a Computer Aided Device, may be berry type operating system.

But a machine is doing something what the man is unable.

Rona is out of these critical question.

He is in deep thought about a more serious matter. His marriage.

He will do this heavy duty just after returning.

Aayna, Khayna also leave the matter upon Bayna, joined to Rona.

Sona is final? Ayna asked.

And Preeti? Khayna knows, there are other candidates also.

When that is Plutonic, you can choose other also.

You don't love anyone.

Love! Rona try to analysis. Failed.

He charged Aayna—you love—

No, see Rona, love and sympathy are not the same—Aayna.

And girls are like flowers, beautiful flowers, they are just to see—Khayna.

Not to pluck—Aayna remind the statutory warning.

You keep the communication with both, Aayna adviced, and one day you will find whom to marry.

Love! Love is above all. Love can do miracle. Bayna believes.

The word has entered to his ear from the gossip.

But love has negative sides also. Destroy many lives.

A scene flash to his brain. The dancing Fau.

Stone statue must not fall in love. But a living element? Fau can be taken as semi living. Or or Bayna's brain never defeats. He got the answer.

May be one living being behind. Possible, very much possible.

Competition of love . . . ok. I shall love uki also

CHAPTER TWENTY

Discipline

There is no God—Pou is sure.

But I have heard of them. They either gift a boon, if you please them-Tou also not in defeating mode.

They were discussing about an old book. 'God—the ultimate machine', a book written in 2013.

They were the saints, but for their restricted life and knowledge, they earn spiritual power—Sou.

And they are termed as—god or—goddess.

If now we can meet such a saint—Nou.

Why?—others.

I have heard a story. Once upon a time, there was a saint, a good saint, blessed all—Nou.

Then?—Tou

One day, a rat came to him, and prayed to make it a cat—Nou.

So that, no cat can eat it.—Pou

Yes, the saint made it cat. After some days, the cat came and prayed to turn it to a tiger—Nou is interrupted by Sou.

But, if we find such a saint, what he will do for us?

He will turn one of us to a small thing, so that we can enter within Uki—Nou expose his plan.

But how do they do that?—Hou, in a disbelieve mode.

If you live a disciplined life, if you never do any harm to anyone, you will gather a power—that is the strength of your mind. You will get what you want—Sou continues,

Because, you will want that thing for the truth, for the better, as your soul is above little interests.

All this talks are for the sweet smell.

Fau is liking Uki.

He often show his dance spreading, swinging his wings.

And the smell is detected frequently.

And the bad smell also, frequently. At their night time.

CHAPTER TWENTY ONE

T A group

Alibaba and the thiefs? Aayna asked.

The Sampan group is at emergency meeting.

Sweet smell is for the CAD berry and bad smell for us? Bayna had taken two days to think and then consult with Jayna.

We must let them know—he told Jayna.

Them means, the control unit of Sampan. Control them from the Earth.

The T A group. The Terrific Aggressive group.

They have landed few hours ago. From the Earth.

Bayna explain the situation.

No, not Alibaba, Bayna is sure. Because, the point came his brain also. And many times he uttered many words.

No, sound operated system cann't be. Total impossible.

Khayna is very excited. With the imagination of huge amount of treasures. The golds, the diamonds, and many others. The glitter is before his eyes. Open the—Khayna's imagination open the door.

Will you keep some for Sona? Khayna whispering to Rona.

Rona, wishing for quick solution, leave the greed. He only wants to end the search as early as he wants. Boring, life is boring here.

They are doing something—Bayna is damn sure. He is angry with himself—as the plan Romance made is not understandable.

Kau, must be Kau—one of the TA group gives his opinion.

They have verified the curve traces of the smell detector. If they can find some other cause.

No, the stones are fond of the CAD berry. Fond of him only.

For this point the TA group is happy, the living objects of Romance has also at their same rank. Failed. Failed to emit sweet smell.

Failed? or they have not noticed? may be ignored—no way to know.

The science behind, Bayna in total silence. He is not interested in side talks. We have to discover the science behind.

Uki must not use the deodorant.

CHAPTER TWENTY TWO

terrific greed

The whole sale hole sellers. The greedy group.

The ta group is the part of them.

They only be the happy, they only be the winner.

For last fifty years, they are after their plan.

In very sugar coated way.

The majority of Iio know them and remain alert about them.

But, everywhere, there are some persons who never take the truth easily.

Some of Iio pampers the ta group.

The ta team dislikes the romance team. Their team members never win to Sou Pou Nou . . .

They, many times go to the shelter of lie to defeat the boys.

Very cleverly, the ta group, has been taking the advantages from the Iio people.

And trying to damage their young members.

By their cleverly, they have earned many thing for which they are not worthy.

The news of Uki was coming to them, from a far. They were some how confused about the genuine elements. The romance boys are going to be the master of such a large wealth!

May be their members are not so brilliant, may be they are not hardy, may be they have not such knowledge, may be they are not so controlled ;

But the wealth will be their.

Sou wants to make them naked. But the matter must come before all. With some witness.

And he got it. For uki.

CHAPTER TWENTY TWO (B)

dingi

Romance group is at diner.
Continues their discussion. The spiritual power.

I have heard if you pray to god with a pure heart, God will gift that thing—Tou.

In ancient time, the earth people did many types of prayer—Kou.

Now, we make never a prayer—Nou.

'cause, we have nothing to pray—Tou. We have everything for need.

What they wanted?—Kou.

Money, jewellery, home—Sou.

Even childs, specially boy child—Nou.

Yes, I have heard about a special child—a million dollar baby. When he was born, the wise told that he will be a very special. He will have the knowledge of all the subject. His father, to please the God Shiva, made worship in different and hard—Sou is fond of telling story.

What type?—Pou.

He prayed to each temple of Shiva, at the side of the river Ganges.

Oh, Indian. They have a habit of worship, specially the Brahmins—Kou.

I have seen the river at the map—Hou.

But why? He is genius by birth. Then again?—Pou.

For his long life, the wise persons knew, there will be many one who will try to make harm him, to destroy his strength.

The same story of all great men—Nou is sad. He was expecting some new.

A beep is coming from radar.

Two dots are over the monitor.

All of them are around the monitor.

Dingi.

They have recognised the small space shuttle from the earth.

Standing at some distance from romance. Very near to sampan.

They have no time to wait. The dingi people.

Within few minutes, they enter to romance.

They are confirmed that romance boys are doing some wrong. Doing something hiding them. They never blame their low level intellect or education.

The fine evening is damaged. By the hot words. Quite cultureless.

The furious expression shattered the romance group.

The cause is beyond their imagination.

CHAPTER TWENTY THREE

the great explosion

They all became statue.
The smell, the sweet smell—Sou broke the silence.
And the bad smell—Pou add.
What?—all together.

Yes, Pou pointed with his finger to the monitor screen. Screen of the smell detector meter.

It is the day time for Sampan. Now they are at the open land.

And trying to making hole here and there.

But how? Hou.

The TA group is a Iio jealous group. They all knew that. They never helped the Iio people for last days. But when Iio people have formed a other world, and developed their system day by day, this TA group joined them.

Why they are blaming us?—Kou asked others. Have we made any harm to them.

When Fou is nearUki, sweet smell is coming, and when other is there, bad smell is coming—Sou is trying to diagnosis the problem.

That's not our fault, nor we have command Uki to do that—Pou is angry.

No, they are asking the scientific cause behind. Actually they want to know about our achievement—Kou.

Actually, they want the fruit—Nou with a cartoon laugh.

In between their conference, Fau alone has gone out.

To check the external side of romance.

The TA group was not very far then. They whispered themselves.

And approach toward Fau. They want to check Fau's uniform.

With spreading the leg, Fau swing its wings.

The TA group members fall on the ground.

Fau enters and lock the door . . . it is the time to sleep.

CHAPTER TWENTY FOUR

classical love

It is their time to sleep. For Romance group.
Before going to bed, they have a habit to chat.
Some days have gone after the attack. The attack from TA group.

They have heard, the TA group left neo that night.

Both the groups are going tired to search the smell and other mystery of Uki in their own day time.

At night, they dislike to discuss about those topic.

They want to relax.

Today's topic was love, the classical love.

They have heard many classical love story of the ancient days. Of seventeenth to twenty first century.

After that, love has gradually diminishes from the life.

They have heard Romeo Juliet.

Very interesting to Pou.

Very boring to Nou.

Probably love is a kind of disease to Kou.

It is the steering force of human being, to Sou.

Love means one boy and one girl and one villain, toHou.

It is a loss of time, to Tou.

But all like to hear it. Apart from their life. They request Sou to tell a love story . . . a special one.

Yes, I have a good story. Very unique story of love . . . a love fantasy.

Name? Nou is going out of patience.

TIME FREEZE

—Sou declared.

It is also a love story. Classical love story. But in another sense. It is not classical for wining over time, like layla maznu etc.

But it is classical, as based upon a classical theory of Physics.

Sou starts the story.

56

CHAPTER TWENTY FIVE

time freeze (I)

Problem is the distance—Sou has started his story. How much? Pou is the problem solver.

Take, million of light year—Sou 's approximate measurement.

Not very much, it can be overcome—Tou, with their own experience.

The distance is in between hero and heroine.

What's their name?—Nou.

Sumansuvra—Sou, it was fixed in his mind.

And the heroine?—all together.

Not fixed, not found—Sou.

Kanchanmala? Kou proposes. At very ancient time, the common heroine for all fantasy.

No, no, very old—all opposes.

Then Kathi, Mily, Liza, ...—the names came in line from them.

Sou—these are very light . . . cheap type.

Gladilova—ultimately, he found.

Suits to classical love, Nou is happy now.

Now, about them. They are very simple . . . nothing extraordinary. In their life style, in their intellect, in their attitude, in every sense.

It is difficult to be ordinary, than to be extraordinary—Pou, from his memory.

They are alike, love needs that—Kou is always serious.

They are alike, as they are both alone, no relative, no friend, pass their days with own.

All show sadness at their mouth.

They are alike, both of them are believe in God.

Which god?—tou asked.

No specific, one who is beside the honest, hardy human, one who likes the human who has no greed, who live a simple life.

You were telling about the distance—Pou remind Sou.

Yes, they are alike but their residence is at two separate planets, very far.

There are no where at this galaxy except Earth and Iio, man live there—Kou,

It's not a reality—Nou, thoughtful about the future of the story.

And the name of the story? why time is freeze?—all together.

That is the story. You will find the justification, at the end—Sou end here.

Chapter twenty six

The Hole Seller

The holes are of heavy demand.

From the twenty first century,
The black holes were discovered at the nineteenth century.
For one century, it was so so.
But, from the next century, the Astronomy gets improved with modern instruments, space programs.
The world found the importance of the black holes.

They get interested how the holes absorb all the colours of light.

What type of gas filled are they? And many more questions.

After the establishment of Iio, the auction started. For the land at moon and other planets. It became the status symbol for the rich.

From few decades ago, the earth people get interested to buy the black holes. As those are subjects of research, not for sell. But as like other property, illegal selling is going. The black marketiers of these hole sale are called by their nick name—hole seller group or HS.

Bayna was thinking about them. He does not suit with other of his group.

Their main group. The so called hole seller group or the HS group.

They govern the sampan group from the earth. Others of sampan are quite simple type. They never involve within any critical problem. Just obey the orders. And pass the leisure in merry, talking about nonsense. Irritating talks all those.

Now, the HS group is Bayna's headache. Only Bayna's.

The group must poke their ugly nose to Uki. When there is a strong smell of something. Probability is high for to be valuable.

It is also in Bayna's imagination. His awaken dream show him precious jewellery within Uki.

Byna want to take the credit. To discover those. To get those.

But, not only the Romance group, there is the HS group. They are more dangerous than Romance. Bayna knows it from the childhood.

Byna is expecting them at every moment . . . low patience greedy people.

CHAPTER TWENTY SEVEN

Milky way

Romance group is also aware of the HS—hole seller group.

They are now on recess. After their duty.

With ferry they are at the sky.

The white sky . . . no smoke, no dust.

Fau Mau are at guard.

With the modern instruments, the romance group is measuring the dimensions of the holes.

Holes are expanding. The gaseous composition is increasing in volume.

The HS group is expecting that, man will get into the very deep region of the holes. The very high temperature zone, though.

Expecting some precious metals or unknown elements.

The astronomy is also curious about the holes. After century years research till.

The holes found have characteristics different at different locality of the galaxy. The scientists found the bunch nearer to the earth as of very low temperature, whereas, those nearer to Jupiter, are very hot. From outermost layer to the innermost. The Romance group drive within this region.

They have found another scoop. Recently. The holes are sold by second hand also. At a low cost. After their search, the buyers sell them at one fourth to one twentieth rate.

The problem is, holes are gone to very common people. The real research work is hampered. The common people spoil the experiments.

The Romance group is at constant watch. They have the information that the HS group make rounds of and on for data.

The HS group is also in contact with the Sampan, the romance team knew it also.

They are flying like the free birds now over the infinite space.

CHAPTER TWENTY EIGHT

time freeze (II)

Gladilova must be of sixteen—Nou knows the love story. He love it.

And Sumansuvra is of seventeen—Pou is sure about the expectation.

The diner table. Fou is near the door. After his diner.

Sou 's story is moving ahead.

No, Gladi is of thirty two (32) and Sumansuvra is of twenty (20).

What—they make a shout.

Quite impossible, an impossible love—Nou is damn sure.

Parents will not allow.

No love with aunty—Tou, placing himself within the story.

There are other problem also. They have grown up at different coordinate system—Sou add.

Like us, different from the Aayna Rona—Nou.

And their growth rate is different. Their 'year' are different—Kou from his knowledge of physics.

Their weight will be different—Tou is very thoughtful.

How the love will be? question from Hou.

By blessing of God—Sou assure them.

Yah, the God has come, within the story, it is not a work of humane—Kou laugh.

Yes, the God has to come. God was watching Gladi for many days. The girl live alone. Very depressed.

Like Uki—Hou. Uki loves Fau—their combined lough.

Sumansuvra also—Nou has a good memory.

He is of single man family, but has friends, pass his life jolly—Sou.

God found the girl over earth. For last twenty years, she is alone. Work hard to maintain his daily life—Sou continues.

Like other fantasy heroine—Pou.

Her only life was the Galaxyscope . . . where he found Sumansuvra.

CHAPTER TWENTY NINE

detective Bayna

Probably its jacket, the penguin jacket,—Bayna has found a clue.

The cad berry has a special jacket, Bayna knew that.

Bayna was dead sure that theHS group will be in anxiety hearing the smell episode.

But it's his duty to report them. They are their boss.

They are repeatedly knocking Bayna and other.

Just few days before, their sister concern TA group has made the place hot. Both romance and sampan like to stay peaceful.

What he was thinking, that came to the mind of HS group also.

Bayna tried to hide and to investigate alone, but become unsuccessful.

You must search his jacket, the HS group ordered Bayna.

Bayna told others.

But they never talk with us—Khayna.

We have to make friendship—Bayna.

So, one fine evening, Bayna went to romance.

With white flag on hand.

Romance group is very pleased with their guest.

Byna make a long meeting.

About nothing. Nothing serious.

Avoid eating. Romance group has a different food habit.

Watching everything, with least importance to Fau.

This task make an entry to the daily routine of the desert.

Sou Nou Pou are friends of Aayna Khayna.

They make evening walk at the desert when romance is on duty with Fau.

Hear the song of Fau, clap to his dance.

But all in vein. No bottle of deo is found at the jacket pocket.

Nor, the trace of the door opened by the kick of fau.

No story of treasure is there.

The romance group ignore Uki, leave Uki for Fau.

Ayna Khayna Rona as a result, now sing and dance with Fau

      5   6   7   8   say us good night

CHAPTER THIRTY

time freeze (iii)

Good night now come with Sumansuvra and Gladilova.

The fantasy hero and heroine.

Sou's story is on move.

The galaxyscope?—Nou is curious.

Yes, next generation of telescope—Pou.

Strong eyesight—Kou.

Gladilova pass her off time with this toy. She visit planets at her wish, Sou continues. The link will vanish for flow of questions.

One day she found Sumansuvra, a good looking boy.

But, he is very younger—Kou again.

In reality, not very—Sou, understanding that here the story require a lecture.

In relativity, not very, if you say more correctly, now Sou is the teacher.

What is time?—Sou.

The fourth dimension—Kou.

And what is relative time?—Sou.

Time at two different coordinate system, moving with a relative velocity—Sou.

As for example?—Hou.

Say Earth and Moon, Earth and Iio, Venus and Neo etc etc—Sou. The span of a day is different at these two places.

As, at Neo a day means six month—Pou agrees.

Its very fallacy—Kou.

No, its fantasy—Sou.

There, the planets are such that, Gladilova is on Earth and Sumansuvra is at a planet revolving with a smaller velocity, Sou returns to the story.

Say X,—a small comment from Tou.

X is such a distance from the Earth that, the time span when Gladilova becomes older by one month, Suman suvra is by twelve year—Sou.

One week means three year, beyond reality—Nou.

Taken granted for love—Pou support Sou.

CHAPTER THIRTY ONE

Calibre

FACE to FACE

Calibre great calibre—Aayna astonished.
Now, romance and sampan are friends.
Ayna Khayna Rona is playing with Tou Kou Hou.
Fou is near uki.
Ayna cleverly proposed the romance boys about a new game.
They will throw their tools to make hole over the stones here and there.
They must call Fau. The hero—keeping within his mind.
Others are ready. And Aayna wins. They call Fau.
Fau is an expert, this type of matter.
Rona does not agree. He wants to show his calibre where his marriage matters.

The game rule is decided. Rank will be high for longer distance.

Tweny meter? asked Tou.

All stand there. Except Fau . . . he has not reached yet.

All win.

They will not call fau. Aayna try to keep the game on.

Fifty meter? Kou Hou Khayna fails.

Hundred meter? competition is now between Aayna and Tou.

Both of them fail. No dust is out from the stone. Their knives do not reach the standing stones. The boundary base of Uki.

But Aayna win. His luck favour him. Fau's mood is changed suddenly.

He run to the group.

Kou throw his knife. Fau follow him. He swings his collar. Collar of the penguin jacket.

The dust fall on the ground.

Ayna's concentration was on Kou's face. He noticed the order but not the collar.

Aayna wants to check.

Calibre, great calibre, will it can from more distance?

Yes, two hundred, five hundred, Fau, go behind—Kou told Fau.

Fau make the action replay from a long distance, almost nearer to sampan.

Aayna has something to tell today. To Bayna. His investigative eye has found the source.

His face remain as it was. Hiding excitation, he claps— really four hundred calibre.

CHAPTER THIRTY TWO

time freeze (iv)

Gladilova, likes to see Sumansuvra. Days after days she spent time with her galaxyscope.

Sumansuvra at his job, Sumansuvra at his rest, Sumansuvra at drive.

Now, everything about sumansuvra is well known to her. His talk, his smile, his walk.

After the question answer session of Physics, the romance group stop to interrupt Sou. Ttoday he is at his flow.

After some months, she became brave. She make a contact. She wants to be friend. Friend of Sumansuvra.

She likes me—Sumansuvra also feeling bore to his single life. Begin to communicate with her.

Like we and earth people—Nou calculate.

Few months went like this. Introduction and then the relationship grows.

Now they want to spent time together.

They plan about that. If they live together, where they will.

If, they reside on earth, she will be of thirty two and Sumansuvra will remain at twenty.

Both of their age will change simultaneously.

She is disliking this age difference. Her culture objects.

If, she will be at Sumansuvra's homeland, then the,

age difference will be jumped—Tou's brain is very sharp for mathematics, he could not stop himself from interrupting.

Time is marching. No path is before them,—Sou.

Gladilova, as like all other problem, started to pray to the god.

She prayed with all her mind, all her honesty, all her discipline.

God always helps them, who help themselves, like Gladilova.

CHAPTER THIRTY THREE

Sampan

Its from his collar—Aayna reported Bayna.

I also thought that—Bayna, now also his eyes is focused at Fau, dancing Fau. Very near to Uki.

But I think, it is from his wings, Rona, with a low voice. Generally, he is sincere to his work. But Fau's performance give him a lot of fun.

May be, may be from both. Bayna back to his table.

He has to calculate . . . the strength of the force striking the stones.

Others are to their whisper.

Jayna, dislike to go outside. Rona, Khayna inform everything to him at night.

They were saying, Uki likes Fau. The words go to the ear of Bayna.

Likes a cadberry? fuhh

She gift the smell—Khayna's analysis. Good for them whom she likes and bad for dislike—Rona, from the experience. He had a number of girlfriends at his homeland.

Is she a living body? Bayna, now with the Physics book.

Probably, the cadberry spray some scent, it was his deduction. From the collar.

But today's game forced him to think in other way.

The matter, whichever is emitted from the collar has a great energy.

Laser? like the laser gun? no, that's not possible.

Uki must be a form of a god, Khayna. Some mythological character. She understand human being.

And make gift in that manner, according to her choice, possible—support from Rona.

If it was laser, Sou must alert other, laser affect human body—Bayna, temporarily returning to other,

See, Khayna, good or bad, will depend on who cares you and who don't.

CHAPTER THIRTY FOUR

time freeze (v)

Then, one day, as like other fantasy, God appear before Gladi.

Gladilova describe the whole incident.

Do you like him? God asked.

Yes, but Sumansuvra is much younger. I am thirty one and he is only twenty.

They both desire to spent some time together. Some days.

Gladi disclose her wish. And also the problem. Where they will live?

The difference will remain twelve, here or there—Nou rectifies the last day answer, I mean on earth or on the unknown planet.

God heard both the problems. Gladi is too good. She never demand anything to God. What she has gained, all from her own effort. For the first time, she prayed to me, something, God agree to help her.

He gave them a boon. The problem solver.

For only one month, one month in his lifetime, Sumansuvra can stay on earth, and his time zone will be as like his planet.

Sou stops at this point, the main point of the story.

Yes, then every thing is all right—Nou is satisfied.

Kou calculates. One week means twelve year.

After one week, Sumansuvra's age will be thirty two and

And Gladi will be thirty one plus—Kou.

And the age problem has solved, Gladi will be junior of Sumansuvra.

But how?—Hou, though it is fantasy. But Sou has a habit to sleep also in accordance to the laws and formula.

The inertia, inertia of time

and will vanish after a week, week of earth—Sou in serious attitude.

CHAPTER THIRTY FIVE

Sampan

It must be the nano waves, Bayna is now sure.

The cause of all calibre. Calibre of that robot.

Bayna has not forgotten the fight. Fight between Fau and the TA group.

Fau alone defeat them.

No, not only for his leg throwing. He found from his memory that Fau was swinging his wings.

And the TA group also felt a thrust of wind.

The stones are cracked also by the same weapon.

There may be some gadgets attached to the nano wave generator.

Whenever it goes to the high tension attitude, the smell emits.

Bayna told Aayna. His detection.

Rose scent with HT? Aayna confused.

And bad smell? Aayna asked.

That is . . . have to think over.

Bayna has taken the decision. He must inform the HS group.

They need such type of jacket.

Need very badly. Because he must discover the treasure within Uki.

Bayna is good at art. He quickly design the jacket.

With the probable gadgets attached to it.

Send to the HS group.

The available tools and weapons will not work. Uki is very hard.

CHAPTER THIRTY SIX

time freeze (vi)

Time is always running . . . it has no inertia,—Pou.

It is not a lazy boy, will make delay to wake up—Nou.

But relative time can have—Sou wish to back to the story.

If you are on a time machine, what will be? You will go to hundred years after and your parents will be at present.

And you will be much older than your father—Kou gives the logic.

That's a game—Nou.

It's a fantasy. Sur Real—above reality, Sou reminds them. And continues-

God gave them the boon.

He told Gladi to spent this one month as her dream.

Now, Sumansuvra and Gladilova is happy.

They are happy for the coming one month.

They don't want to think about the days after that.

Gladilova spent her days by tailor work.

With a low income.

Sumansuvra decides to help her.

For some days they make many plan and make the corrections.

And, finally, the blue print is ready.

They will make this month colourful. No black and white shade.

They will spent each week at separate shade.

Each week, Sumansuvra will be three years older—Pou interrupted.

By the inertia of time, for him, time will run with the velocity of his planet.

The difference will decrease after every week, interesting to Kou.

Now, Sumansuvra is at earth and beside Gladilova. They are starting their first week . . . conjugal first week.

CHAPTER THIRTY SEVEN

LP Ji

Sending the penguin jacket information, Bayna wished to visit Uki.

Till now, he never dig. That is the job of Aayna Khayna.

Some time will be required—he told himself, to prepare the special jacket.

It is the day time for sampan, and night for romance.

Now, Neo is at such a position that the Uki side is towards the Jupiter and the rasa tree region is towards the Sun. This winter continues approximately six month. It is the middle of the winter. Here temperature is, Bayna noticed it before coming out from sampan.

Minus thirty degree celsious.

Bayna reach Uki in slow walk.

Rona Khayna Aayna are searching on other part.

Till now, nothing has been found by either team except this stone.

Jayna is engaged to the experiments at the lab. To find the breaking point of the stone.

Dynamite will be required, think Bayna.

If no door is found, we have to create the door. And before the romance.

Romance has helped them in many ways. They also donate the penguin jackets from Iio. Otherwise, this tour was not possible. It is impossible to live at this temperature with the all human accessories.

Cheating the cold is not so easy.

But, Bayna is firm. He will not share anything which he will get from Uki.

Bayna is watching Uki closely.

Yes, Fau stands here. Bayna can not dance.

Before, his further action, he heard a girl voice—'L P Li' 'L P Ji'

CHAPTER THIRTY EIGHT

time freeze (vii)

This their first week. Sumansuvra and Gladilova's.

It is the sunny days of the country where Gladi lives.

The fungi colour sea is before them. It is one of the most attractive beach of this continent. Miles of length.

At this early morning, beyond the lines of coconut trees, the sea seems more tranquile.

The hut is just behind them. These seven day's residence.

This beach is quite lonely. Tourists generally gather at other beaches . . . the island has a no. of beaches.

Here, no shops and market nearby.

Sumansuvra and Gladi both like silence.

They have reached here three days ago.

There are two water scooters at the edge. After breakfast, they will drive over the sea. Gladi is very glad.

At her village, she, many time, pass her time before the show of the swan, swimming over the pond.

Now, they are the swan of the sea.

Most part of the day, they are at the sea.

Sumansuvra cross the crest easily and with high speed. His skill is high.

Gladi remains at a distance behind.

Sumansuvra returns, drive slow, keeping pace with Gladi.

They drive far and far, till the beach vanishes from their eyesight.

With the setting sun, they run over the golden sand. Chase one another.

A huge amount of coloured shell is now at Gladi's collection.

Sumansuvra catch some crabs. It will go to their diner table.

Gladi is a good cook. Crab bar-b-q—not bad.

They share their past at night. At the lantern light.

Sumansuvra becomes more sad, more sympathetic compairing the two.

They plan their future three weeks.

CHAPTER THIRTY NINE

life partner

L P Ji!
That means—
Life partner ji mr. life partner
The young stars talk like this.

The disection is going on at sampan.

Bayna gets afraid, just afraid, hearing Uki's voice.

Ran back to sampan.

His excited talk tell the story.

Aayna help him to understand.

A stone can not talk—Jayna.

But I heard clearly—Bayna in defence. He is not at all lunatic about Uki. Like that cad berry.

The romance group have not hear any sound till now.

Sentence is almost beyond imagination, huh, Rona himself.

Bayna always try to get importance, it is his opinion.

Gas may be out from a cave, it may be Visuvious or Fujisan but it talks! Aayna told other.

He wants to be hero, Rona's mute words, and
Like a heroine—with a volume to the group.

Bayna dislike the comparison. He is disliking the whole thing. Except a chance. A chance to get the mystery solved.

You may be wrong. Sometimes it seems someone is talking nearby . . . though none is there. Our subconscious. This come within our thinking deep—Aayna tries to make the matter cool.

But the whole group is shakened. Another mystery.

The smell detector shows the existence of sweet smell.

When Bayna was there.

CHAPTER FORTY

time freeze (viii)

God is a machine, how can he bless us—Hou asked Sou.

For the last episode, they never interrupt. Today they are in rapid revise.

In ancient time, human beings imagined god is also human with super power, super intellect.

But, in twenty first century, S.A.B named one shows, God is the ultimate machine, a never ending running machine, a universal administrative unit.

At this, twenty sixth century, Nou Hou Kou . . . know God in that sense.

When, the machine rotate in that direction, that you are benefited, that will be the blessing of God, Sou wishes to be out of debate and to enter the story. Others also.

Now, Sumansuvra and Gladilova are passing their second week, Sou started.

And Sumansuvra is of twenty three, reminds Pou, the calculator.

Yes, a bit grown up, but much younger than Gladi, Sou continues.

They are on their way for the second week. On last week, they agreed to be farmer. For that, their destination is at the hills.

The hut, the sea beach, the scooters all left behind.

Sumansuvra wishes to change the profession of Gladi, he wants to see Gladi as a farm owner, a farm of spices.

It's the rain at the mountains. Time to plough.

Sumansuvra is driving casually. Their farm is at a distance.

The sea beach is beautiful, but the hills are more, Gladi feels happy.

And their farm with the cottage is more more.

Men are already at work there, the plants from nursery have taken their place. With the rainbow at back of the cottage, they entered.

Gladi dislike to take help, but this time is different.

Just a luck try, good company brings the heaven—she heard the proverb.

CHAPTER FORTY ONE

Hero

Fau was the hero, Khayna is not happy. He likes Fau.

Now here is another hero.

Trace of sweet smell for a sampan member is a turning point.

Uki has sixth sense. She wants the match ends with a tie, Rona thinks.

He does not bother about any sound or any smell.

He has got the opportunity to visit light years, gather some experience, it is enough for his small life.

No, now must be serious about the matter, Aayna proposed to others.

Bayna is already very serious.

His report to HS group contradicts this.

They have to change the plan, he share with Aayna.

No, these two are separate issue. For the defence mechanism we have the Fau jacket, Aayna always at cool brain.

A perfume bottle and a recorder, are enough to deviate us from our work, Aayna disturbed, as already Uki becomes a fantasy to many of us.

We are walking far from reality, he said.

Yes, we have to search these things, Bayna back to reality.

But we are searching for all these days, Rona is bored.

The desert map is before Bayna, his fingers point over it.

No door, now there is no confusion, we have tried 'open the sesam' with all types of energy, not only the sound, Bayna eliminates one possibility.

Then, only, Aayna bend over the map, nothing is there, except,

Yes, he has got it, the clock, the grand clock, the necklace.

He point his finger over the watch, without voice.

May be, there are space within it, Bayna congratulate Aayna for the detection. Resolution comes to check the clock from tomorrow.

Uki likes Fau, Uki likes Bayna, Uki likes both? Khayna dislikes.

CHAPTER FORTY TWO

time freeze (ix)

No, love must be one directional, and love must be reversible, Sou advice the junior.

At the break within the second week story, some dispute arises.

No love scene, Kou asked Sou.

Discussion shifts to the theory of love.

No, they are just friend, just good friend, Sou explain.

Boy friend of Gladi, Nou corrects.

The boy is crossing his boyhood.

Their morning starts with the late sun rise of the hills, the border of the valley.

The plants are very rare, very costly, need high level care.

Gladi keep watch on every one.

They are growing with Sumansuvra.

Dates? they did not make dates? Kou asked.

Looking at Sou's face, Nou changed the words—dates are found at the desert, they are desert tree. They are planting spices. Spice, rich spicy food, you will get it at Asia.

Next time, we shall collect some, Pou ends.

Whether, I alone, can manage? Gladi doubts. Her mind always remember her that these days are not for the whole life.

She is very choosy. About attachment.

She is very sensitive also.

One man, may be of high quality, has no bad habit, learned, but not to her liking, many time occurs this, for nails, nor unbrushed teeth, for unnecessary long hair etc etc.

Her friends advice her to make robot as she like.

Lastly, I have to accept that, she had taken for granted.

Till now, she has not found any such point in Sumansuvra.

Who is now with the musical instrument, to compose some new.

With the dusk and the moon, her eyes follows the finger,

Follows hands, face, eyes, hair, then lips.

Call of the lips . . . . irresistable Sumansuvra singing a very old song, at a low volume.

CHAPTER FORTY THREE

the clock

The clock is atomic clock. Accuracy is of nanosecond order.

The basic theory was invented at twentieth century.

For two century, used for micro fine experiments at laboratories.

The time duration to reside at the unstable state when the atoms are excited, and the time duration to be back to its original state is utilised for these clocks—Bayna explain to other.

But, I, calm down very quickly, and Rona, if anyone taunt him, remain in angry state for many hours—Khayna makes problem.

Are all atoms are alike? Aayna simplifies.

No, Khayna, no, atoms are like us, their behaviour are separate for different identity—Bayna teaches,

Then? Khayna, how the clocks will give accurate time?

Simple, calibration, if one use you, the excitation time divided some minutes that much your excitation time will be second ; and for Rona, divided by some hours—Bayna.

But, as here accuracy must be hundred percent, scientists can not use I, you, he, she ; they utilise highly cool brain some atom,

Now, the picture almost clear to the sampan boys.

But, Bayna continues, they return to their place, but there must not be hidden anything within the actual clock, it will be within the casing.

The casing with the large display has enough place to keep recorder or other thing.

Now, they are sure, it is the work of the naughty romance group.

Must be the remote controlled gadgets to make them afraid.

The clock is at a high. Aayna, Bayna, Khayna are good at mountaineering.

So, no problem.

Operation necklace—tonight or today, whichever you say, fixed.

CHAPTER FORTY FOUR

mountaineering

S weet smell! and Fau is here! the romance group astonished.

Few days ago, they found the trace of sweet smell at their smell detector, when they were at rest.

The sampan has one whom Uki likes. Now, they are in the fantasy mood.

Sou did not take the matter so lightly. He was watching the sampan group.

Tonight, after the fantasy period over, Sou and Pou are beside the window.

They are enough wise to get the plan of the sampan.

Aayna, Khayna, Rona, with their mountaineering cords and hooks, at the base of the statue. Others are at a distance.

These guys are guided by the HS—Pou, only Bayna is somehow different.

Sou is watching their steps. They are good mountaineer.

The case is locked, but they can unlocked it easily.

Watch, the pendant, is not at very high. Three reaches there soon.

Opened the case.

No, noh, nothing is there.

Their finger signed negative mark to Bayna.

Hopeless, he knew, they cannot. He instructed to check more.

Will we bring the watch? Khayna asked. They are sure, there is nothing, and they are sure about Bayna.

Bayna, show negative mark.

May be, they got the clue, and take away the spray at their day time—Bayna thought.

Thief—Bayna heard the word clearly. Uki called him thief.

CHAPTER FORTY FIVE

time freeze (x)

A nything for your smile—Gladi uttered silently.

She, had scrutinize Sumansuvra. Everything is allright, like many other young, but his physique differs, and his smile. Gladi dislikes muscles, again dislike thin body.

Probably, this is for the milk. Gladi has allergy to that. Several times, Sumansuvra asked for a glass.

Their third week started.

Sumansuvra is now of twenty six. His smile remains same, but attitude turns towards more serious with the chick and chin.

The plants are grow up. One or two are flowered.

These flowers are the raw spices.

Sun above at the clear sky are soft, the peaks are grey. Morning needs some woollen. The best atmosphere.

Gladi is glad.

Though it is the hard time. Any negligence will cost a much.

Each plant is under their observation.

The fruit spice will come some days after.

Fencing is with rare hilly sky reaching trees. They are also costly.

Gladi learnt a lot for these two weeks. About the scientific nursing of the plants . . . these type of sensitive plants.

These days are out of phase from those at the sea beach . . . but she is liking. Now she is not alone.

Am I fall in love with Sumansuvra? I must not . . . this is a dream. And dream is dream. Gladi talks with herself, with the selection of fertilisers, pouring water to the roots, measuring the heights of the plants, cutting the branch and leaf.

What is in his mind? She does not know. They talk about the days past, about the plants, about the import export, about storage ; but not about themselves. They heard about their relation from the others surrounding.

We will shift to the city next week. You can not live here alone. And you have to make the business. It will be easier at the city, Sumansuvra show the advice her, at the poolside tea time.

Anything for your smile, she knod to permit.

CHAPTER FORTY SIX

drastic

Greed results death—greed results death—

The sound is clear . . . byna's ear is of high resolution.

It's uki.

They have returned to sampan.

No, nothing, all of them, anyone are not lucky like byna.

But, total impossible, they have searched the watchcase, nothing is hidden.

And, uki speaks only with me.

But, today is a bad day . . . to the boarders of sampan.

Byna informd the hs group, about the jacket . . . jacket of fau.

It must be short waves . . . the collar and the wings have the transmitter attached . . . wave transmitter . . . the intensity are different.

The area covered are also different.

Byna heard about the high tension . . . the jacket has the source of high tension signal generator.

Probably, very small size nuclear battery.

Byna's report covered all this.

They were expecting to receive a duplicate from the earth.

After a month, they have received the answer.

The earth people are unable to prepare the duplicate.

They have failed to attach the gadgets, even to a ordinary jacket.

No alternate way, other than to theft it . . . uki will be their.

CHAPTER FORTY SEVEN

time freeze (xi)

But age does not matter to love—Pou.

Sou is busy. For some days, Sou remain busy most of the time.

Others are chatting. About the story.

Now, it does not matter—Nou, but that time it matter.

How?—Hou.

Tradition. It was the tradition that bride will be younger than groom.

Physiological cause—Kou, seriously.

Not physiological, mental, men can not live without woman, but woman can live without man—Nou, in wise mood. Man wanted to die before.

There was other reasons also, Pou add—financial. That time women was financially dependent. Tthey were married at lower age. Scenario changed when ladies become also earning members.

Anyway, this is granted,—Kou.

Next, why spices? There are so many things,—Tou. They did not take spicy food.

Those time, spices were the most costly. Man must gift something precious to his girl friend—Kou's analysis.

Dates? it will also romantic. The tree will give birth one for the first date, two on the second . . . imagination of Pou.

No, see, this is not Arabian, this is Mughalian, Gladi will cook biriany,

With the spices from their garden—Kou justifies.

Yes, where we were? Sou asked others.

At the end of third week. The spice has just to come—Tou.

Sumansuvra is of twenty nine—Pou.

Now they will shift to the city, they have decided—Kou.

Yes, and it is also, the last week will be colourful—Sou.

CHAPTER FORTY EIGHT

automatic Fly

A utomatic fly—we shall use it.

One member attached to HS group suggests.

Hs group has landed some hours before.

It is determined to take off the jacket from Fau.

Bayna is happy. That will be his. Others can not operate the gadgets.

Fau never swing his collar or wings before Uki.

The HS group will make the door with this. Door for treasures.

Bayna is excited. Others also, for the incidence.

Whether they will succeeded?

The fly is automatic. Remote adjust its height of fly according to the target.

And will spray chloroform finding the target—Fau.

Bayna will take the jacket then. The plan is solid.

Every one is ready. Aayna will keep watch. Khayna and Rona will bring Fau out of romance at their evening time.

The special evening. Sau leaves Fau with Khayna, Rona. Aayna stands near romance. If anyone will be out, he will ring the alarm. Bayna, behind Uki, hiding, ready for the moment.

Bayna makes the power on.

At this moment, Fau is waiting. Rona, Khayna have gone to nature's call.

At some distance. Others of the group here and there.

Gone, gone above Fau's body. The automatic fly, flied four hands above fly.

Timely, very much on time, Fau lied over the ground.

But, not in absolute vein, the plan succeded.

The fly has strike the target. Whom it found first at his path.

It's Sweta—a member of HS group. Curiosity turns to curse. She was came running, overconfidence about their pet.

CHAPTER FORTY NINE

brilliant bee

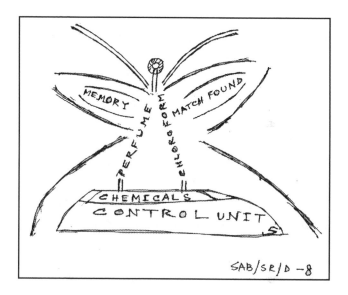

L et's play a game—Sau suggest.
Sumansuvra and Gladi are on the way of their colourful life.

And, at this time a game, and, by God, it is with those sampan boys.

Yes, when they are so close to us now, let's make a friendly match.

Next day, Sau placed the proposal to the sampan boys.

A kabadi type game. Romance versus sampan and their guest.

—Sau knows who within the camp.

They have nothing to deny. They have to hide the failure, and to return their request.

The time is fixed at the day time of sampan.

The game starts. One of this team will chase one of other, out on touch.

They have started to enjoy the game, throwing off the hesitation.

No, these boys are not bad. But they are rich. Rich in intellect.

The whole desert is populated today. Even Fau is also running.

Sound is not heard here, but everyone's face is full of laugh.

Not a bad idea, Pou Kou Nou also feels, a good change.

But the bee.

One bee has entered to the field.

Firstly, Bayna. He felt sleep over the ground. All are busy to win.

Ayna, Khayna—and then HS6 has understand, something is happening.

The bee is now near Pou, then Nou. They are at motion as they were.

Now, it is near Jayna, he fall on ground.

Remote, remote—HS10 shows his intelligentia.

All the romance boys are at the field and playing. Who is operating the remote? The bee is flying in all directions.

It is a strong rose perfume, but how? Hou search for his team members.

They are gathered near Uki. The sampan boys with their guest are all in sleep.

They will be wake up after some time don't worry.

Sou, Kou is laughing. Just a return—no one must hurt Fau.

But how?

A simple self guided system. Recognise friend or foe. Brilliant bee.

CHAPTER FIFTY

timefreeze (xii)

H ou mou khou manusher gandhya pau

It is a code from Fau to alert romance. About some external body, migrated to the desert.

Sou and Pou found Dingi—the space ship of the hs group.

And from that moment, they became busy. They had sense the problem.

Sou shows the fly episode to others, leaving the sampan boys at the desert. All of them were in deep sleep.

Now, the boys want the story. For some days, Sumansuvra and Gladilova remain at a halt.

Today, they are towards the city.

Putting the black and white off.

The garden of spices is very rich. They have made the security.

Matured Sumansuvra is now twenty nine. Responsible face.

They will be at the city, to set the marketing system of the spices.

With the star crowded clear sky of winter, they are on the way.

From the next visit, Gladi will be alone, at the garden, at the cottage.

She have left her nearer many one, experienced in life, single life,

But can she come back, she asked herself.

But this is a blessing, like a special dress, like a special diner, like a festival tour.

Yes, it is like a tour. We met many unknown unidentified and after days they turn to memory.

Sumansuvra will be a memory, a precious memory.

CHAPTER FIFTY ONE

sampan

All the sampan members are in lord Buddha form. Sitted over the white sand. Bewildered.

They have woke up minutes ago.

No sign of the romance boys.

They are in deep sleep. Its their midnight.

Silently, sampan boys and guests return to sampan.

They were ready—Aayna.

The sampan group is not liking this.

They are here for discovery, for science. To make their carrier.

These HS people is spoiling the aim.

What was happening? Aayna asked?

Probably chloroform, for us—Bayna has found.

And, for them?—Khayna, how the bee identified them?

It's brilliant, not only automatic—Bayna explained.

The automatic devices was invented at the end of twentieth century. As for example, an automatic iron. It can sense the heat of the cloth. Going beyond the specific temperature, it will be off automatically.

It is like that Rona possess—Khayna.

But, it can not sense the type of texture—cotton, nylon or poly; you have to set the limiting temperature accordingly. But when the gadget will be brilliant, it will set self and will be auto selection type.

I shall have one like that—Khayna. It will distinguishes me from other male.

CHAPTER FIFTY TWO

time freeze (xiii)

Tragedy, then it's a tragedy—Kou uttered.

Sou, on continuation to the starting of the last week.

That will be decided at last scene—Pou. He wants the story.

Yesterday, both have reached to their city house.

The city is new to Gladi. A nice city. With clean roads, gardens, parks and business provisions. A rich city. Gladi will stay here, as per wish of Sumansuvra, and will supervise her farm, not very far.

With the beautiful balcony, the house attracts Gladi.

The first day, they have spent to decorate it.

It was a different colour of daily life. Gladi feels, like a family.

Today, on the second day, they have changed the mood.

This evening, in their romantic mood.

They are walking on the pavements, towards the lake.

Both are well dressed. Shifted from the morning balance sheet,

Walking with the jolly and joky words.

Like cinema, in reality, the full moon is behind them, following them.

Irresistibly took me to the pole

Under the dessert soft moonlit, at the lake side restaurant, they end their diner with the hot coffey and the rhythm,

Swinging vibrating

CHAPTER FIFTY THREE

the parity

D evlina Sangeeta Fultuci Fulti Shukla Ushakanya Choudhurykanya

Nou Pou Hou are uttering the names. Names of the blackholes.

Magha Ashlesha Atri Bashistha

Sou is showing the stars. The stars of importance.

Tabuma—Pou shows another blackhole.

After that game, and after many days, the romance boys are at sky!

Flying with their single seater formula one space vehicles—ferry.

Swati, Kou pass a blackhole, without touching.

When the HS group is here, they must make the number increase by new invention.

Sou points at far—a red dwarf.

It may turn to a blackhole—Tou ask.

May be, I have not such depth—Kou answered.

They are driving very carefully . . . otherwise, may be fallen within the holes. Unlimited in number in this zone. And some have strong magnetic power within them.

A little mass from star run flying within the group.

This may reach to Iio, may to earth, Nou make the imagination.

Can kiss fly? Can kiss fly within vaccu?—Hou asked.

Why? Sou.

No, we don't know whether Sumansuvra had send kiss to Gladi before their live together.

CHAPTER FIFTY FOUR

time freeze(XIV)

No, no scene of kiss, they are traditional.

Today is their third day of fourth week.

And Sumansuvra is twenty nine years ten months eight days twelve hours, Pau makes a pause within the story.

Yes, and one hair may be found grey—Kou

Sau did not pay any importance to them. This is not maths time.

Now, Sumansuvra is setting the business scheme for Gladi.

On day time, they are searching the market for export of the spices.

Gladi is good cook. On the first day, she made some special dishes.

Sumansuvra helped her. He is also habituated.

They fixed their menu returning from the collection of raw materials.

Total veg? special day, special dish and no non veg?—Nou dislikes.

But today, Sumansuvra planned for an outing, for the rest of the day.

At the lap of the mountain. The mountains are covered with velvet grass.

They took two horses. Gladi likes the white.

With the gallop of the horses, their meaningless and no connection talks were moving. About the rebels, once upon a time, who hide within these valley. The granite walls are such constructed at this range, that the place turns to a fort.

Gladi makes an imagination—if Sumansuvra and she was of that time, if Sumansuvra was a rebel!

Village at a far, they halt for meal. The sun is almost on departure.

No left right, they turn one eighty degree, towards their home.

CHAPTER FIFTY FIVE

dhumaka

They are going beyond—Sou thought.

A small toy plane is flying round romance. Sou knows, there is camera attached, spying over them.

They have made the beech of contract, Sou discussed with Pou and Kou.

Their eyes are at the plane.

The plane vanishes. They laugh. Again it appears

They keep on watching.

Remote controlled—Kou, being happy.

Before, the sampan group reached here, a pact was made, no one will spy over other ; no one will disturb other, no one will depend in any way over other. And, in other cases, their normal penal code will be followed.

So long, the sampan group was alone, there was no problem.

But this hs team—all fraud, Sou think.

The lesson was not enough—Kou understand.

No, but we shall not attack them. Make them a game—Sou.

They have lost the last day—Nou hear the word game.

The romance team spread over the desert. Only Sou and Kou remain.

Sou set the frequency tracer. After some trial, he got the desired.

The hs team found a similar plane to fly around their camp.

Member 1 ran after that, member2 tries to catch that.

Bayna, on the recorder, was checking the data send by their spy, shouted—link fail, link fail. Their spy has betrayed.

The romantic spy is now crawling round the hs team.

Chapter fifty six

time freeze (xv)

What they had taken at that village?—Kou fill up the gap.

The hill village type food, Sou answered.

Sumansuvra and Gladilova, both like simple life, and self dependent life. So, they can accommodate themselves, Sou on the mood of story teller.

Gladi, being a woman of that time, likes freedom, and self dependence.

She, after the plan was made about their business, decided not to take any financial help.

She was learning every small to smaller part of the business.

The flowchart is made.

Now, some times will be required to ripe the spices.

Those will be brought to the city, and will be export item.

Sumansuvra is now a serious teacher. He is now about thirty one.

Gladi, being a student was observing him.

Sumansuvra is not like other young. He is very matured.

Gladi returns to the lake side, under sky restaurant. The conversation was very little.

But, they were, beside other.

Yesterday, on the third day of this week, they were back, the green mountain was on one side, the river is on the other. The two horses was walking in slow motion, as they were friends like them.

Gladi was feeling, she can live the rest of the days with the memory.

Memory of these few days.

Some one says, she interrupts to the flowchart, to live one year is more than to live hundred years.

Yes, but, if you do some thing rare, something unique which will make you immortal, then.

Gladi returns to the names of their staff, who will help her. From the lake.

What was their menu their?—Nou.

Who paid the bill?—Kou.

CHAPTER FIFTY SEVEN

smart spy

They will not supply us the drink.

An emergency meeting is held at sampan.

By any mean, they failed to make the special jacket of their own.

And there is no easy way to win Uki.

Bayna was imagining the jewels and bezels within the cave.

He can not loose.

The last way is the missile—hs member 3 gives the verdict.

And Bayna found, the link has failed with their spy.He shouts—link fail.

Everyone makes a round around the screen. No picture is on the screen.

All look out of the windows.

A toy helicopter is flying around sampan.

As they look at it, it lands over the ground and crawled.

Bayna, with an angry face, turned to hs members.

The noise waves. They are throwing the noise waves.

Our spy remote is not working.

The hs member direct Bayna—the same weapon.

Bayna, set the signal generator.

Instruct to produce noise signal.

No effect.

The romantic spy keep on flying as it was.

CHAPTER FIFTY EIGHT

timefreeze (xvi)

Are you ready? Sumansuvra is calling Gladi. Don't be late, it is a long way.

Gladi, quickly, finish her dressing.

Today, they plan for an outing to a local fair.

A fairy fair—Pou gives the pause.

Gladi likes these fairs. She likes to see varieties.

They starts to walk, joining with many other.

The Mahabharata is going on open stage.

That time, drama meant Ramayana Mahabharata to the village people.

Those are fatty books. I had find it at the heritage—Tou is proud.

Shops are the main attraction of a fair—Kou add.

For some time, they became the audience of the open stage drama.

Then they search for 'out of routine' snacks. These are mainly available at these fairs.

With the tribal dance, the snacks suits well.

Touching the stone temple, they return to Mahabharata.

Ultimately, no one gain anything—Gladi make the dialogue within Bhim's (a prominent character).

These cases end like this—Sumansuvra, experienced from practical life.

With a bite to potato fry.

They shift to the toy gun practice.

You know, proposal of my first arrange marriage was made by elder brother, with a tribal boy—very simple, blant, our neighbour, Gladi recollect her memory from the tribal dance.

They were planted by the zaminder of our village. To serve him.

But, in times, they, even the girls became Government servant.

And the marriage?—Sumansuvra is curious.

Bad luck favours . . . in turn, I also fixed his cousin for my elder brother.

And, both of them show no interest about us.

But, they were our good friends.

The whole place is covered with addicting tribal flower odour.

These atmosphere always carry Gladi to her childhood.

A far away from her present. But Gladi need not any sympathy from anyone. She is well, very well.

With all the crowd, she also turn jolly.

Collects the glass bangles, tribal shawl and jacket.

Probably, this day will not return, not probably, she is sure.

Evening turns dark. Time to back to the civilized known regular scenes.

Leaving the war of dialogues of Kuru and Pandu, they end their fourth day.

Only three days left.

CHAPTER FIFTY NINE

cold war

And our drinks—Khayna again asked.

The smart spy had vanished.

Noise signal has no effect on it.

Not remote operated.

The hs group is at the edge.

The spy has recorded all our talks—member 3.

They are now informed about the missle.

Ayna Khayna are happy. This hs group is making problem one after another. They were happy before dingi has landed.

They are not so much interested about the treasure of Uki.

Khayna, already was being ready to supply the news of missile to the romance group.

The smart spy has done his job.

For the last few days, they were helping the romance.

Now, we must not waste our time. We must not make them preparation.

They will inform Iio, the arms will be brought, and before that we shall quit from here.

All we? Bayna asked. And their research! And why? The romance will not be here. The full kingdom is there. No Fau, no romance.

And Uki is his! A doubt arise within his mind. He knows this group.

The target?

Uki—member 1, determined.

Ukiiii full sampan cried.

CHAPTER SIXTY

time freeze (xvii)

After many days, a good dance performance.

Gladi likes dance, Sumansuvra song.

They are coming out from a cinema hall. The fifth day's program.

A world war time romantic film.

Gladi heard the war from her father. Her grand father was bounded to join the second world war, being a higher rank British government officer. He was posted at that Mesopotemia, now the middle east.

Head of the main postal system, and hence, he had to operate one such office from the war field.

That time communication was not so strong like now. The telegraph was the only way.

May be, but I have heard from my father, the communication was not so poor. One of our leader deliver his speech from Japan. And you know, the v of Churchill? That's a very interesting story. The media forced him to tell the position of war ships. That was a great plan of Hitler, if Churchill denies, that will prove the defeat of the alliance.

Within few minutes of his answer, the ships were drowned.

Communication was not poor.

Hitler, if he was not so eccentric, world may get a great administrator, Sumansuvra 's opinion.

Yes, but mental clot is very bad. His clot was the parents. Why he will not also have a good parent. Others happiness, specially family happiness was intollerable to him.

Yah, the maximum crime occurs for lack of love, the feelings that when no one loves me, no one will get it, Sumansuvra joined to Gladi.

Am I love you? Gladi asked herself. No, her brain is stronger than heart. She will love after her marriage. Am I like you?

CHAPTER SIXTY ONE

Einstein

Anger and hate have no fate

Nou sings in between.

Right, he lost all the precious.

The most famous scientists are from Germany.

The most research done during world war. Mainly of physics.

For Hitler, they fled to America one after other.

The name and fame goes to America. All the benefits also.

Einstein was one of them. His theory of relativity is quite attached to this story, Sou in discussion with others.

To describe the position of anything—I, we, he, she ; we need a coordinate system. Each heavenly body in motion have separate coordinate system.

As like the planets—Nou interrupts Sou.

Yes, and the coordinate systems of different planet are in relative motion.

The general physics takes the mass of any body is absolutely constant over the whole universe, and all laws were formulated by taken it as granted. But Einstein told, the mass changes when the body is at motion.

And the change ratio depends on velocity.

In derivation from Einstein's relation, scientists show that the dimensions—3 space coordinates and time also changes with the velocity of the coordinate system.

And then the problem of age comes—Pou concludes.

Yes, but the question is—which two planets or satellite may have this age ratio? Sou place the home task.

CHAPTER SIXTY TWO

protocol

Love	like	pity	hate
	No date		no date

The romance boys, like the old times, again at the white ground.

Fau is dancing before Uki.

They know the sampan is watching them.

They know the hs group is being ready with the missile.

They know the target is Uki.

No drink, no drink—Kou with the same tune.

As per pact between the two expeditor groups, romance supplied the rasa drinks.

With their play and work, they are discussing the fantasy.

Jews—the most intellectual race, I have heard—Pou.

Hitler hate them, for their prospour, for their innovation—Nou.

Like the common people—Tou, being the philosopher.

For his jew father, for whom he was identityless, refuged—
Kou, the senior. This type are egoistic, power greed is the
main stirring of life . . . always try to make others slave, to
be rich,

Rich with others property, like the hole seller gang—Hou
interrupted.

The romance team is acting, as they are going on
unprepared.

Sou, specialist of self guided system, is busy with his, job.

Uki must be full secured.

CHAPTER SIXTY THREE

timefreeze (xviii)

Profit, what is about profit?—Sumansuvra makes the question, to Gladi.

Today is the last by one, Sumansuvra has crossed thirty one.

Now, Gladi does not feel the discontinuity of age.

The morning is their busiest morning.

Sumansuvra, last time checking about the business.

Gladi can handle smoothly.

Gladi was engaged in cooking.

A party is called, at their home.

All those, whom Gladi will work with are invited.

Some, from their farmhouse will also join.

Gladi, from last night planned the menu.

No profit, for me, Sumansuvra pinch Gladi.

Gladi concentrate to the home decoration.

The dinner table is ready. She put the wine glasses.

A good health covers many thing, for a man, Gladi is impressed to well dressed Sumansuvra.
Healthy diet and disciplined life gives a good polish, she appreciate.

Guests started to join the party with the evening.

Sumansuvra introduced one another.

After a small meeting over the process, with the drinks, all request Sumansuvra for a song.

Leaving the vodka upon the table, Gladi plays the tune on piano chord.

Sumansuvra has the words

Signal interpreted by heart

Lips receive,

Response due for the meeting.

After the thanks giving slot, for the special buffet of spicy and tasty dishes, the guests make the good bye, to Sumansuvra.

They heard, Sumansuvra will be back to his home, a far away from here.

Response due for the meeting

With the disappearing structure of Sumansuvra, Gladilova tries to imagine the days of her single life, again.

CHAPTER SIXTY FOUR

READY STEADY

Tomorrow will be the last day, for all we—hs member1 verdict,

And we need not any rasa drink, member 2 conclude.

All we? Khayna dislikes. But there is no alternate.

If Uki is destroyed, they will have no job here ; and the Iio people will be their enemy, Aayna quickly calculates. Whether the sampan will fly before the attack?

No, you will have to wait, we have to collect the matters inside, member 3 is guiding the sampan.

Rona, Khayna remain silent.

The missile—hs group possess is a guided surface to surface. It burst whenever it strikes an obstacle.

The hs members are in action, to fit the missile with desired projectile angle and direction, from the missile base on dingi.

Bayna, at sampan, ready for taking data, at his lab with all instruments.

Rona started to weep. He can not bear the death of love.

Fau loves uki.

Khayna Aayna try to make him cool.

The missile may be wet.

It may burst before striking.

The angle of projection may be incorrect.

If the members of hs group sudden attacked by diarrehia.

Success of all possibilities are feeble. If Uki can run away.

CHAPTER SIXTY FIVE

time freeze (xix)

L ips sound love
I doubt

Sumansuvra composing.

Only few hours left.

The o'matsury (festival) will be over.

The fantasy is ending with tragedy.

But they can marry, now Sumansuvra has grown up—Pou,

Yes, Nou they know each other—Nou.

And there is no villain—Kou.

The queue of question march towards Sou.

Sou is cool. Sumansuvra is grown up, they have passed one month with other, now they know what food they like, what dress they like, what time table they like etc etc.

Sou answered as he is completing his exam papers.

And, the only villain is the time. They got these days as a blessing.

Only for one month. The time is frozen for Gladilova.

And on move for Sumansuvra.

That will be a problem—Nou is very thoughtful. What will be their next forth dimension if they live at earth there is problem, and if they both shift to Sumansuvra' residence—that will also be a problem.

A real villain—al lare morowsed.

Love can overcome that, Sou returned to the story. But actual problem is,

All are eager—

They have not reached to that critical point—point of phase changing.

CHAPTER SIXTY SIX

the gas

Only Fau can collect sweet smell—Hou in failure.

And for all of us, the bad—Kou.

No, the sweet smell is for Bayna of the sampan also—Aayna remind them.

The sampan team except Bayna is here. At romance.

The plan is of hs member4.

To watch the romance, to engage them in themselves.

Disgusting—Aayna pronounced before leaving sampan.

But nothing to do, these people will not let them live unless they hear.

All, with their snacks, at the round table conference.

They are very eager to know the fact, about the gas.

It's for their height—Sou discloses.

All they know what is waiting to happen, but shows no anxiety.

Height? how?—Hou.

You all know, light gas moves up ; keeping the heavier below. Fou and Bayna is a slight bit of more height than us.

But the smell?—Nou, weak in chemistry.

The organic gases has aroma and of lighter than inorganic—Sou.

And the many inorganic are of rotten egg type—Pou, remembering the smell.

Benzin and Ammonia—Tou find at last.

May be, something like those—Sou, in hurry moves inside, he have to cook for the guest.

CHAPTER SIXTY SEVEN

timefreeze (xx)

FANTASY

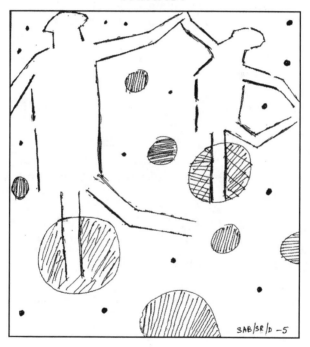

M L—sou announced.
My love—pou.
No, my life—nou.

A spherical crystal with two words engraved—m l,
Sou described.

A farewell gift from Gladilova.

Last night, Gladi could not sleep. Whole night, she prayed to her god.

She knew, this one month is like a celebration, never returned ceremony. But, heard to bear.

God hear her. On the early morning, she found the crystal with the blessing—this will make you together.

The whole day, they passed in heavy weather at their home.

Though, Sumansuvra, with his song, tried to make it light.

After their last diner, Gladi present her gift.

Sumansuvra, with his rare smile, and with his new composition

I can not betray my heart

Surprised Gladi, a gift in return,

Three words G M L holding a diamond, a pendant.

The romance team claps all together.

And Sumansuvra vanishes within the dark.

The end of the fantasy—Kou declared.

No, the starting of another—ANABAS, the NON RESIDENCE.

CHAPTER SIXTY EIGHT

the grand finale

Hashi, with a pair of hashi (chopstick), Sou returns from the kitchen.

All were waiting with curiosity.

And the LPji? All in same tone, just at the entry of sou.

Bayna found it. He is alone at the sampan. At the control desk of their missile. It will strike after just few minutes. From dingi—the space ship of the hs group.

A small bright light is progressing towards dingi.

The hs members are in count down, 10 9 8

Signal from Bayna . . . a missile is at the screen, some hundreds of meters from dingi . . . danger signal for hs team.

Dingi was ready to fly. It was waiting for the hs missile projection.

No time, dingi takes off with all their arms and gadgets.

Sou shows his finger over the radar screen. Aayna Pou Khayna Kou Rona Tou Jayna Nou all bend round over the screen.

Dingi and one fire stick at it behind.

Aayna astonished. Own missile? Is it a boomerang?

Nohh, it is from romance. And from the kitchen.

All follow the show. HS members are clever. They drive dingi behind romance.

The sampan team run towards the door. For safety.

Sou make them cool.

The intelligent missile turns a bend and fly at the back of the romance.

At the shoulder of dingi.

CHAPTER SIXTY NINE

FLUTE

The flute technology.

After the grand obituary of the hs group, some days have passed.

The shakened system has returned to the set up.

Romance and sampan—both team has returned to their normal routine.

Sometimes members visit to other.

The intelligent missile had the target—dingi.

It found dingi—hiding at the backside of romance.

The ashes of dingi with their members still now over the white ground behind the romance.

May their soul rest in peace.

The black holes will be sold again—by other sellers.

But romance and sampan are again at their mood.

Today, at the finishing of the story.

That is the flute technology—Sou explains. The gas comes out by fine bores, it will make sound nearby if air or other wave vibrates.

The phase and frequency is set such, it will sound L P ji— like do re me.

I made it for bores at height.

They can laugh as Bayana is not within them.

He is with his repentation—I should object the missile.

He is at his study table, Uki is before his eyes—other side of the window. He is searching the syllabus of love.

Only a lover can be the achiever.

CHAPTER SEVENTY

curtain drop

The brilliant bee is flying all over the white desert.

Today it is spraying the perfume only.

Today is the party day.

The penguin party.

The white desert is covered with big small, high short penguins.

The foods are ready at the tables in between.

The circle with one mile radius is lightened island within the total dark surrounding.

Romance and sampan are standing at the boundary.

With Fau as show stopper, they started the party dance.

For today, they have left the tragedy of Sumansuvra and Gladilova at a side.

All may be true except the inertia of time—Pou makes the conclusion to Sou at a break.

But physics support these—Sou also not to go back foot.

Time has no lethargy, time always march with time—Pou is wining.

And we have also to give it company—Sou directed all to end the ceremony. Let us follow the time!

END

List of topics under research of the author

1. nuclear battery
2. the penguin dress
3. the gadgets attached to the dress—nano wave emitter
4. the cadberry os—biobot
5. self controlled gadgets—a. brilliant bee, b. smart spy c. intelligent missile
6. application of classical dynamics in fantasy

All patents of these items and all copyright to mention these to other books or films is reserved by the author.